# Road Signs

Written by Tracey Michele

# Picture Dictionary

curves

dead end

no parking

Read the picture dictionary. You will find these words in the book.

one way

speed limit

stop

Look at this road sign.
It tells drivers to stop.

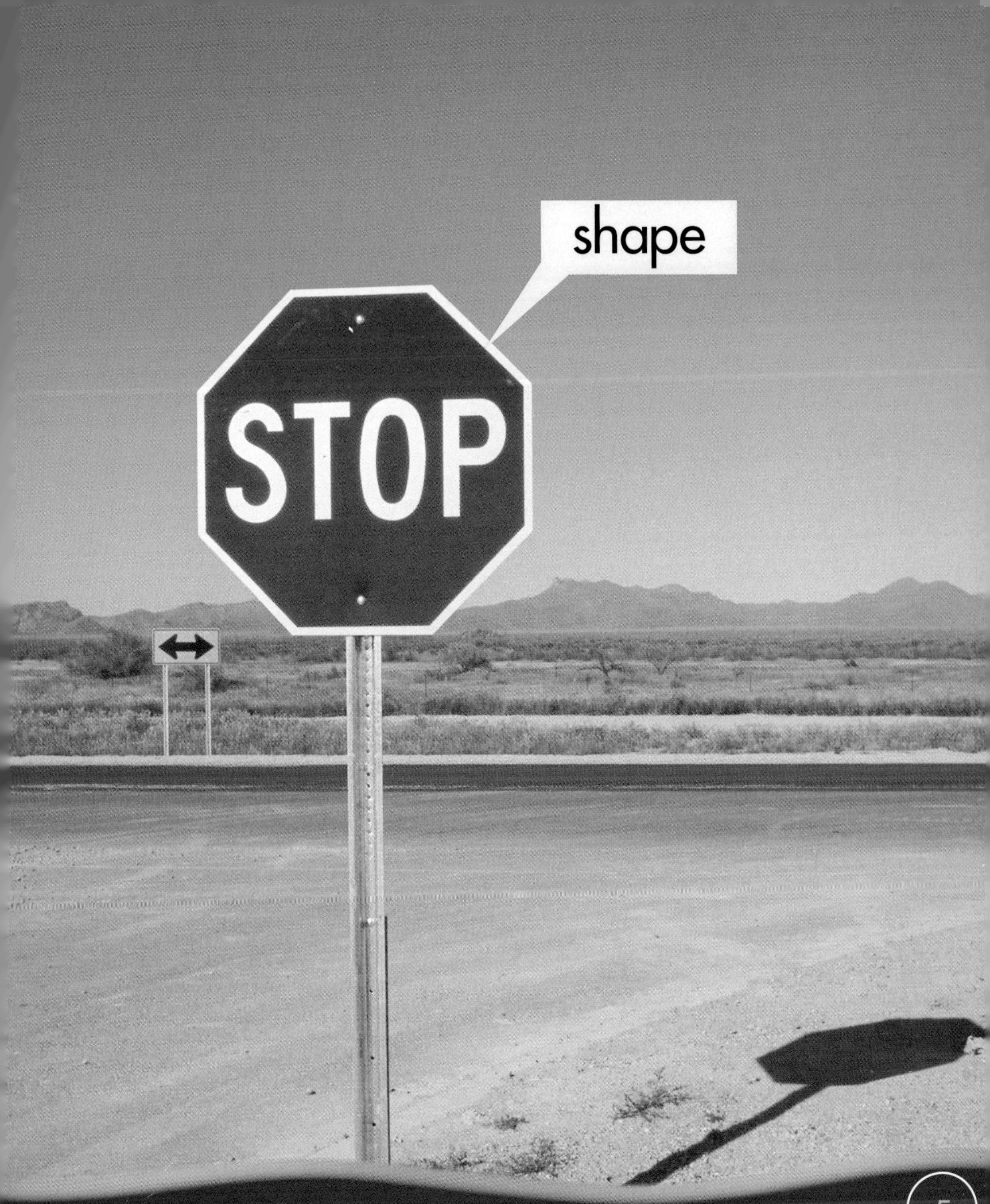
shape
STOP

Look at this road sign.
It tells drivers
that the road curves.

symbol

Look at this road sign.
It tells drivers
how fast to go.

SPEED
LIMIT
45

number

Look at this road sign.
It tells drivers
which way to go.

ONE WAY

arrow

Look at this road sign.
It tells drivers that
there is no way through.

words

DEAD
END

Look at this road sign.
It tells drivers
not to park here.

line

# Activity Page

1. Draw other signs that you know.

2. Write captions that tell what the signs mean.

Do you know the dictionary words?